Joseph's Other Red Sock

For my son Joseph

Copyright © 1982 by Niki Daly

First published June 1982
Second impression July 1983

British Library Cataloging in Publication Data

Daly, Niki
  Joseph's other red sock.
  I. Title
  823[J]   PZ7
  ISBN 0-575-03008-9

Printed in Hong Kong by
Mandarin Offset Ltd.

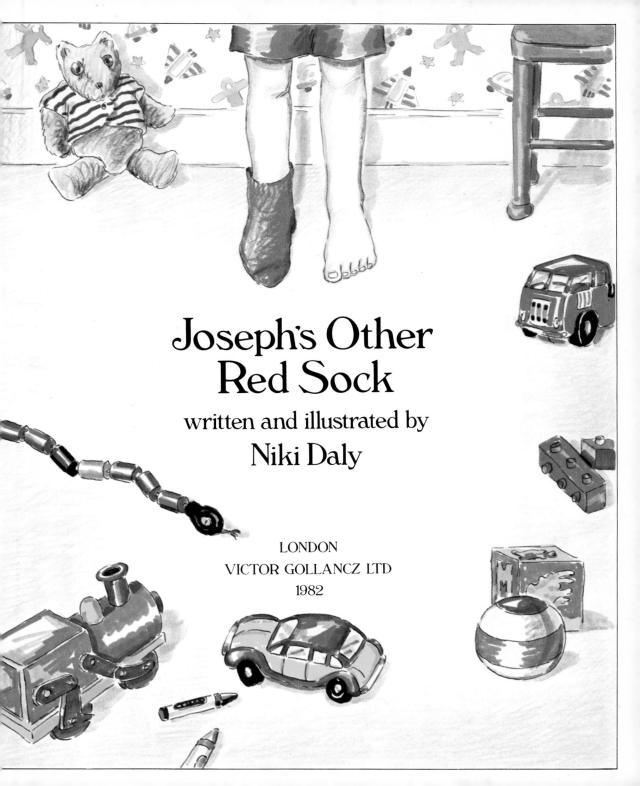

Joseph's Other Red Sock

written and illustrated by
Niki Daly

LONDON
VICTOR GOLLANCZ LTD
1982

"Joseph!" called Mum. "Are you awake?"
"Almost awake," Joseph yawned.
The sun was shining on the wall, toast
was burning and Mum was singing to the
music on her transistor radio.

"Joseph!" called Mum. "Are you spick 'n dandy?"

"Almost," said Joseph. "I'm wearing my T-shirt, and my blue shorts and one red sock."

"Why only *one* red sock?" asked Mum.

"I can't find the other one," said Joseph.

"Have you looked in the laundry bag?" asked Mum.

"Yes," said Joseph, "but I could only find Arthur."

"Did you look in your toy box?"
asked Mum.

"Yes," said Joseph, "but I could
only find Harold and the rabbit with
one eye."

"Did you look in your cupboard?"
asked Mum.

"Yes, I did," said Joseph.

"And what did you find?" asked Mum.

"Something funny," Joseph giggled.

"Funny nice or funny horrible?" asked Mum.

"Funny long and wiggly," said Joseph.

"I hope you didn't touch it!" Mum gasped.

"Yes, I did!" shouted Joseph.

"Oh, Joseph!" Mum said. "And what
happened then?"

"I PULLED!" yelled Joseph.

"And Arthur pulled!
And Harold pulled!
And the rabbit with one eye pulled!"

"And it flopped and flapped and wiggled and jiggled!" shouted Joseph.

"Oh, Joseph!" Mum said. "And what did it look like?"

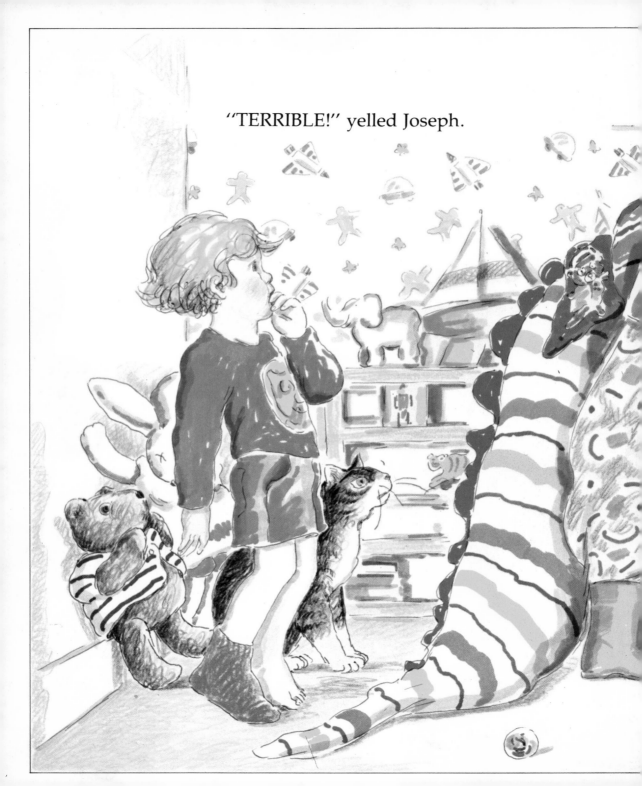

"TERRIBLE!" yelled Joseph.

"And Joseph," asked Mum. "Were you *very* scared?"

"Almost scared," whispered Joseph.

"And what did you say?" asked Mum.

"I said, *'Give me back my other red sock!'*" said Joseph.

"And what happened then?" asked Mum.

"It jumped on top of the cupboard," said Joseph. "And I grabbed its tail. And Arthur pulled. And Harold pulled. And the rabbit with one eye pulled."

"What a lot of pulling!" said Mum. "And did you pull it down?"

"Yes," said Joseph. "And we chased it back into the cupboard."

"Good," said Mum. "That's where it belongs. And what about your other red sock?"

"Well . . ." said Joseph, thinking for a while. "I said, 'Give me back my other red sock *or else*!'"

"Or else what?" asked Mum.

"Or else *I'll fetch my Mum*!" shouted Joseph.

"And did that do the trick?" asked Mum.

"Yes," said Joseph proudly.

"Is that the end of the story?" asked Mum.

"Almost the end," said Joseph.

"Well?" asked Mum.

"It has left an awful mess," said Joseph quietly.

"But what about you, Joseph?"
asked Mum. "Are you all spick 'n
dandy?"

"Almost," said Joseph as he put
on his other red sock and . . .

one blue shoe.